HE'S GOT the WHOLE WORLD in HIS HANDS

KADIR NELSON

Dial Books for Young Readers New York

He's got the whole world in His hands,

He's got the whole world

in His hands,

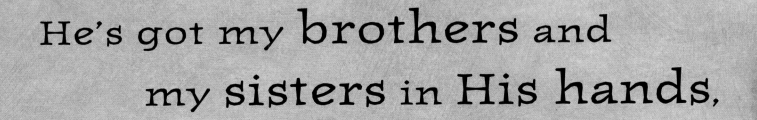

He's got my **brothers** and my **sisters** in His **hands**,

He's got the whole world

in His hands.

He's got the
sun and the **rain**
in His
hands,

He's got the
moon and the stars
in His hands,

He's got the
wind and the clouds
in His hands,

He's got the
whole world
in His hands.

He's got the **rivers** and the **mountains** in His hands,

He's got the oceans and the seas
in His hands,

He's got you
and he's got me
in His hands,
He's got the
whole
world
in His hands.

He's got
everybody
here
in His
hands,

He's got **everybody**
there
in His hands,

He's got everybody

everywhere

in His hands,

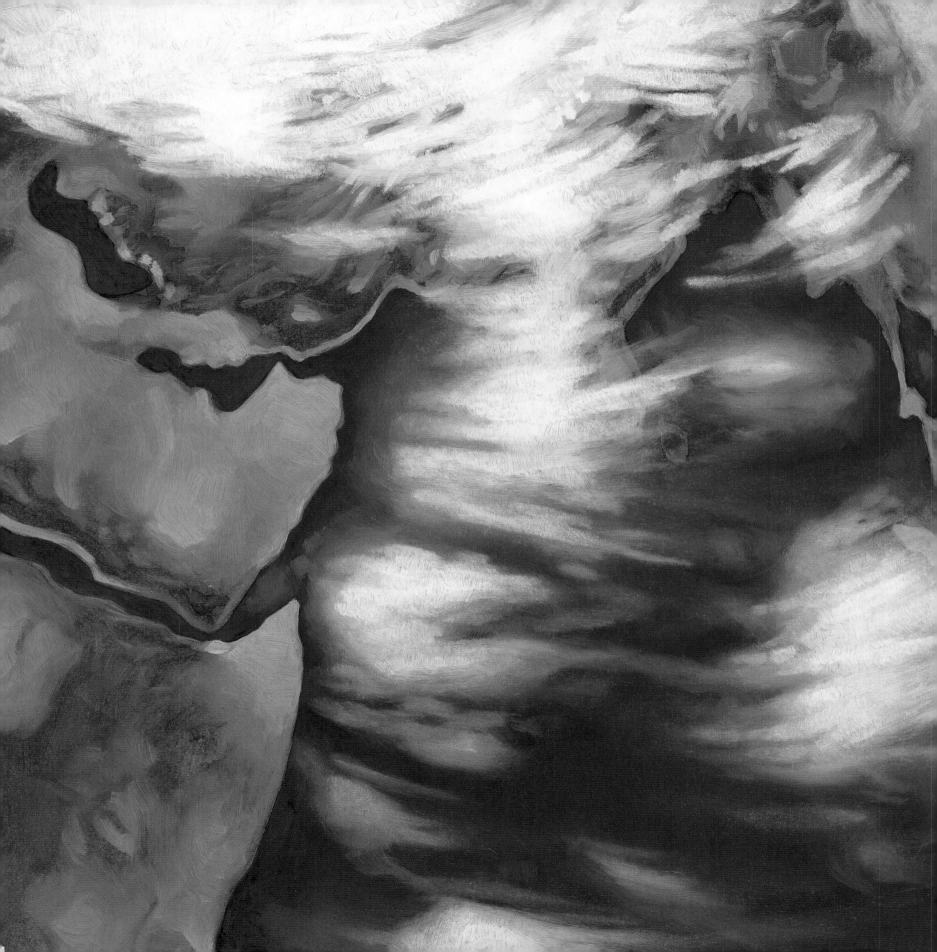

He's got the whole world in His hands.

HE'S GOT the WHOLE WORLD in HIS HANDS

With spirit

1. He's got the whole world _____ in His hands __ He's got the
2.–4. (see additional lyrics)

whole world ____ in His hands __ He's got my broth-ers and my sis - ters __

in His hands __ He's got the whole world in His ___ hands.

2. He's got the sun and the rain in His hands,
   He's got the moon and the stars in His hands,
   He's got the wind and the clouds in His hands,
   He's got the whole world in His hands.

3. He's got the rivers and the mountains in His hands,
   He's got the oceans and the seas in His hands,
   He's got you and he's got me in His hands,
   He's got the whole world in His hands.

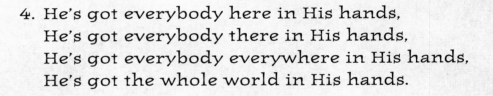

4. He's got everybody here in His hands,
   He's got everybody there in His hands,
   He's got everybody everywhere in His hands,
   He's got the whole world in His hands.

For my wife, Keara.

You mean the world to me. I love you dearly.

A NOTE ABOUT THE SONG

The spiritual "He's Got the Whole World in His Hands" is one of the best-known songs of all time, sung at churches, schools, and camps throughout the country. Who created the first version of the folk song is unknown; often it is attributed simply to "various," as spirituals are songs that have been passed orally from person to person or group to group and improvised along the way. Now there are many versions of the lyrics; the ones chosen for this book may not exactly match those that you yourself know. But the mood and message—that of faith and the importance of community—are the same. The inspirational content of spirituals was crucial to the slaves who created them, and from this musical tradition was born gospel, blues, and jazz.

Over the years, "He's Got the Whole World in His Hands" has been recorded by numerous artists, from opera singer to country star to children's performer, including Marian Anderson, Perry Como, Odetta, Nina Simone, Mahalia Jackson, Loretta Lynn, and Raffi. It even became a number one pop single for a thirteen-year-old boy named Laurie London in 1958. Now this timeless song, still evolving, has also become a picture book.

DIAL BOOKS FOR YOUNG READERS
A division of Penguin Young Readers Group
Published by The Penguin Group • Penguin Group (USA) Inc., 345 Hudson Street, New York, NY 10014, U.S.A. • Penguin Group (Canada), 10 Alcorn Avenue, Toronto, Ontario, Canada M4V 3B2 (a division of Pearson Penguin Canada Inc.) • Penguin Books Ltd, 80 Strand, London WC2R 0RL, England • Penguin Ireland, 25 St. Stephen's Green, Dublin 2, Ireland (a division of Penguin Books Ltd) • Penguin Group (Australia), 250 Camberwell Road, Camberwell, Victoria 3124, Australia (a division of Pearson Australia Group Pty Ltd) • Penguin Books India Pvt Ltd, 11 Community Centre, Panchsheel Park, New Delhi-110 017, India • Penguin Group (NZ), Cnr Airborne and Rosedale Roads, Albany, Auckland 1310, New Zealand (a division of Pearson New Zealand Ltd) • Penguin Books (South Africa) (Pty) Ltd, 24 Sturdee Avenue, Rosebank, Johannesburg 2196, South Africa • Penguin Books Ltd, Registered Offices: 80 Strand, London WC2R 0RL, England

Copyright © 2005 by Kadir Nelson
All rights reserved
Designed by Teresa Kietlinski
Music set by Robert L. Sherwin
Text set in Journal
Manufactured in China on acid-free paper
10 9 8 7 6 5 4 3

Library of Congress Cataloging-in-Publication Data
Nelson, Kadir.
He's got the whole world in his hands / Kadir Nelson.
    p. cm.
ISBN 0-8037-2850-6
I. Title: He has got the whole world in his hands. II. Title.
PZ7.N434457He 2005
2004023075

The artwork for this book was created with pencil, oil, and watercolor. The kid-drawings were created by the artist (using his left hand) with colored pencils.